"Honor your father and your mother ..."
—Exodus 20:12

ZONDERKIDZ

The Berenstain Bears® Show Some Respect
Copyright © 2011 by Berenstain Publishing, Inc.
Illustrations © 2011 by Berenstain Publishing, Inc.

Requests for information should be addressed to:

Zonderkidz, 3900 Sparks Dr. SE, Grand Rapids, Michigan 49546

Library of Congress Cataloging-in-Publication Data

Berenstain, Jan, 1923–
  The Berenstain Bears show some respect / by Jan and Mike Berenstain.
      p.   cm.
  Summary: Brother and Sister Bear are reminded of the importance of respecting
their elders when they set out for a picnic with Mama, Papa, Gran, and Gramps.
  ISBN 978-0-310-72086-7 (softcover)
  [1. Respect—Fiction. 2. Picnicking—Fiction. 3. Family life—Fiction. 4. Christian life—
Fiction. 5. Bears—Fiction.] I. Berenstain, Mike, 1951- II. Title.
  PZ7.B44826Bjv   2011
  [E]—dc22   2010027037

Editor: Mary Hassinger
Art direction: Cindy Davis

Printed in China

17 18 19 20 /DSC/ 22 21 20 19 18 17 16 15 14 13

The Berenstain Bears.
Show Some Respect

written by
Jan and Mike Berenstain

Living Lights™
A Faith Story

ZONDER**kidz**

It was a beautiful summer morning and the Bear family was going on a picnic. Mama and Papa packed up the picnic things. Brother, Sister, and Honey were very excited. Grizzly Gramps and Gran were coming too.

"I made a pot of my special wilderness stew for the picnic," said Gran.
"Mmm-mmm!" said Gramps. "Wilderness stew—my favorite!"
"Yuck-o!" muttered Brother. "Wilderness stew—not one of my favorites."

Sister laughed.

"What was that, Brother?" asked Mama.

"Oh, nothing, Mama," said Brother. "Come on, Sis. Let's pick out a good picnic spot."

The family headed down the sunny dirt road
to find the perfect spot for their picnic. Sister and
Brother ran on ahead.

"Wait for us please, cubs," said Mama. But Sister
and Brother paid no attention.

"Hmmm …," said Mama, none too pleased.

"I remember a good picnic spot right in these trees," said Papa. "We used to come here when I was in school."

"That was about a hundred years ago," said Sister.
"It's pretty run down now. Let's find a better spot."
"Hmmm!" said Papa, none too pleased.

"I know a lovely spot down by that pond," said Mama. "Papa and I came here on our first date."

"That was an awful long time ago,"
said Brother. "It's full of mosquitoes
now. Let's find a better spot."

"Hmmm!" said Mama and Papa,
none too pleased.

"I recall a time when Gramps and I had a nice picnic on top of Big Bear Hill," said Gran as they went on their way. "There was a lovely view, and ..."

"Now, Gran," interrupted Mama. "We don't want to climb all the way up Big Bear Hill. Let's find a better spot."

"Hmmm!" said Gran, none too pleased.

The Bear family trudged across the countryside. They were getting hungry, hot, and tired.

"I have a good idea for a picnic spot," said Gramps. "How about we all ..."

"Now, Gramps," interrupted Papa. "We don't need any help—we know what we're doing."

Gramps stopped short.

"Now, just a doggone minute!" he said. "It seems to me that you folks aren't showing much respect for your elders."

"That's right," agreed Gran. "Brother and Sister are being disrespectful to Mama and Papa."

"And Mama and Papa are being disrespectful to you and me," added Gramps. "You know, us old folks know a thing or two. As the Bible says, 'Age should speak; advanced years should teach wisdom.'"

"But, Gramps!" said Papa.

"But me no 'buts,' sonny!" said Gramps. "'A wise son heeds his father's instruction,'" he added, quoting the Bible, again.

"Sonny?" said Brother and Sister. It never occurred to them that Papa was someone's "sonny."

When they thought it over, Brother, Sister, Mama, and Papa realized that Gramps and Gran were right. They were being disrespectful.

"We're sorry!" said Brother and Sister. "We were excited about the picnic and forgot our manners. We'll be sure to show more respect from now on."

"And we're sorry too!" said Mama and Papa. "We know we shouldn't speak to our elders that way."

"That's fine," smiled Gran. "All is forgiven. Now come along. Gramps will pick a good picnic-spot for us. He's Bear Country's foremost picnic-spot picker-outer."

"Yes, indeedy," said Gramps. "Besides, if we leave it up to all of you, we might starve!"

"Where are we going, Gramps?" asked Brother and Sister as Gramps led them across the countryside.
"Never fear," said Gramps. "Grizzly Gramps, the picnic-spot picker-outer, is here!"

They marched over hill and dale, through wood and field.
"Now there's the perfect picnic spot!" said Gramps, at last.
"But, Gramps!" said Sister. "That's your own house."

"That's right, young'un," he smiled. "Didn't you ever hear of a backyard picnic?"

Gramps and Papa got the grill fired up and they added honey grilled salmon to Gran's wilderness stew.

"Mmm-mmm!" said Brother and Sister. "Honey grilled salmon—that's our favorite!"

They raised glasses of lemonade to Grizzly Gramps, the eldest member of the family.

"To Grizzly Gramps," said Papa, "Bear Country's best picnic-spot picker-outer!"

"You know," said Gramps, as he dug into a big helping of wilderness stew, "it's about time I got a little respect around here."